SNOWMEN
ALL YEAR

Caralyn Buehner

pictures by
Mark Buehner

**Dial Books
for Young Readers**
an imprint of Penguin Group (USA) Inc.

Readers, see if you can find two ducks, a Tyrannosaurus Rex, a rabbit,
a cat, and at least one hidden snowman in each painting.

DIAL BOOKS FOR YOUNG READERS
A division of Penguin Young Readers Group
Published by The Penguin Group
Penguin Group (USA) Inc., 375 Hudson Street, New York, NY 10014, U.S.A. • Penguin Group (Canada), 90 Eglinton
Avenue East, Suite 700, Toronto, Ontario, Canada M4P 2Y3 (a division of Pearson Penguin Canada Inc.) • Penguin Books
Ltd, 80 Strand, London WC2R 0RL, England • Penguin Ireland, 25 St. Stephen's Green, Dublin 2, Ireland (a division of
Penguin Books Ltd) • Penguin Group (Australia), 250 Camberwell Road, Camberwell, Victoria 3124, Australia (a division of
Pearson Australia Group Pty Ltd) • Penguin Books India Pvt Ltd, 11 Community Centre, Panchsheel Park, New Delhi - 110
017, India • Penguin Group (NZ), 67 Apollo Drive, Rosedale, North Shore 0632, New Zealand (a division of Pearson New
Zealand Ltd) • Penguin Books (South Africa) (Pty) Ltd, 24 Sturdee Avenue, Rosebank, Johannesburg 2196, South Africa •
Penguin Books Ltd, Registered Offices: 80 Strand, London WC2R 0RL, England

Designed by Lily Malcom
Manufactured in China on acid-free paper
10 9 8 7 6 5 4 3 2 1

                    Library of Congress Cataloging-in-Publication Data

Buehner, Caralyn.
  Snowmen all year / by Caralyn Buehner ; illustrated by Mark Buehner.
       p. cm.
  Summary: A child imagines what it would be like if a snowman, made of magical snow,
could be a companion throughout the year.
  ISBN 978-0-8037-3383-1 (hardcover)
 [1. Stories in rhyme. 2. Snowmen—Fiction. 3. Year—Fiction.] I. Buehner, Mark, ill. II. Title.
  PZ8.3.B865Sm 2010
  [E]—dc22
                              2009051658

The art was prepared with oil paints over acrylics.

To Joyce and T

I love to build a snowman
On freezing winter days.
But when the sun is bright and warm
My snowman melts away.

There's nothing but a puddle
When my snowman disappears.
If only he were magic
And could stay with me all year!

I'd teach him how to fly a kite
High above the trees;

Then we would dig for pirate gold
Or sail the seven seas.

I know that he would love to see
The tigers at the zoo;

And at my birthday party
We would celebrate *his* too!

We'd go on all the wildest rides
At the amusement park,

But best of all would be the fireworks
Lighting up the dark.

On stormy evenings I would play
My favorite games with him;

On sunny days I'd teach him how
To dive and how to swim.

On summer evenings in the dark
We'd chase some fireflies,

Or sleep out in the quiet woods
Beneath the starry skies.

At the beach we'd play all day
(He'd get very sandy).

We'd trick-or-treat on Halloween
And bring home lots of candy.

Maybe this is magic snow
That will not disappear,

And this snowman will be the one
To stay with me all year!